I Told You So

Lenora (Lenny) and Michael A Yenny

Printed in the United States of America

ISBN 978-1-958434-94-9 (sc)
ISBN 978-1-958434-95-6 (hc)
ISBN 978-1-958434-96-3 (e)

Library of Congress Control Number: 2023911227

2023.06.21

MainSpring Books
5901 W. Century Blvd
Suite 750
Los Angeles, CA, US, 90045

www.mainspringbooks.com

I Told You So

In Arkansas, down in the Ozark Mountains lived an old man. He was kind of a hermit and lived by himself. He made his living by carving critters and even sometimes his own image from the cedar limbs and branches he found lying around. He was tall and thin, had long white hair and a long white beard as well.

His name was Lem and he had a dog named Toby who was always with him. He never cut down a tree. He always said that trees were the life of the Ozark Mountains. Whenever he told you something he would always say, "Now just remember, I told you so."

Winters weren't ever too harsh, and he warmed his little cabin with the broken limbs of the trees that were not suitable for carving. Whenever there was an ice storm, he was always the first one out, checking the trees he loved. Sometimes ice would form on a tree and cause it to split.

Lem would be out early in the morning saving as many of the trees as he could. Even though he wasn't a young man, he was an excellent climber and could climb to the top of most trees. He carried his tools tied around his waist, and would trim out all the split branches and broken limbs. It really broke his heart when every now and then he couldn't save a tree and it had to be cut down. He always saw to it that the wood always went to a needy family, but it seemed that he grieved for the fallen tree.

He would drag branches and limbs back to his little cabin. He always had a big pile that surrounded it. When he wanted to carve, he would go out and look over the pieces carefully, choosing the pieces he would carve.

Then he would say:

"Well, you will make a nice carving of this old man or a nice raccoon, or maybe a rabbit" or whatever he saw in that piece of wood. Then he would sit right down, and the magic of his carving knife would work away. When he was done, he would hold it up and look at it this way and that way and finally say, "See, I told you so."

Once a month or so Lem would bring all of his carvings to the general mercantile to sell. The mercantile was owned by a little woman named Lou. She would put Lem's carvings on a shelf and then pay Lem for the pieces she had sold. Lem would then purchase what he needed to live: always two sacks of flour, a sack of sugar, food for Toby and a few other little things and sometimes a shirt and socks. He only bought what he needed, and he always bought a jar of Lou's homemade jam.

STORE

He would look around before he left and would say to Lou: you should get some of this or that for your store and remember when it sells real well that I told you so. Lou never charged Lem anything for selling his carvings. She had already figured out that Lem had a knack for always being right. She must have heard him say "I told you so" a thousand times, but he never said it like he was better than anyone else. He just said it.

When he would meet folks on the street outside of Lou's store sometimes, they would tell him something like: "Hey Lem, remember when you told me to soak my corn before I planted it so it would sprout faster and the crows wouldn't get it, well, you were right."

Old Lem would just smile, shake his finger and say, "See, I told you so."

On his way home he would always stop along the way, and whatever money he had left he would pay to have all of his carving knives sharpened by the local Forge. Lem could really sharpen his own knives, but the Forge and his family were really poor, so Lem always stopped.

He'd say, "I told you so; that knife didn't hold its edge."
Then he would sit down at the grinding wheel and teach
the Forge a little more about sharpening knives.

He was also teaching him how to shape and fire new knives.
He told him: the more you learn how to do, the better you
will do.

The Forge's wife would always give Lem a sack of fresh
eggs and he'd be on his way.

Before he got to his next stop he would hear "I TOLD YOU SO!"

The widow Jones's children were running and hollering down the road,

"I TOLD YOU SO, LEM'S COMING!"

The two young ones crowded Lem 'till he got to the widow's house. There he gave the widow Jones one sack of the flour, the eggs, and the young ones already had the jam all over their faces.

Then he would sit down on the stoop, pull out two pieces of wood, his carving knife, and begin to carve a little critter for each of the children. They each already had a substantial collection. The widow Jones had been busy and soon had a fine meal made with the flour and eggs.

She even had a nice chicken stew cooking on the stove. Old Lem had told her last time to put a few of these fresh eggs in a warm spot and maybe she'd be surprised. Well, she was because now a few new chickens were scratching around her meager garden. Lem just laughed and said, "see, I told you so."

When the hearty meal was done, he went along home telling the children to do their chores and to help their mother. He also told them to take good care of all the carvings he had made for them.

"Someday," he said, "they'll be worth something, and remember when that day comes just remember, "I told you so."

He went along his way with a loaf of the good widow's bread tucked in his bag.

Soon the widow Jones had quite a flock of chickens and Lem was taking his eggs home after his trip to town. He still stopped to see the children and carve another critter for them, and to eat the wonderful meal the widow Jones always prepared for him.

The Forge was busier too. Besides shoeing horses, he had become the best sharpener of knives in the whole county. He and his family had even opened a little store to sell the fine knives he also made. Lem still stopped to visit and watch the goings on.

He would smile, nod his head, and even if he didn't say it, you knew what he was thinking.

No one ever seemed to notice that Lem's visits to town were getting fewer, and that his walk had slowed, and sometimes he even used a walking stick. Toby too, was not as frisky as he once was and preferred to lie by Lem's feet.

Then one winter, no one saw Lem for several months. You know how people are; busy with their own lives. When spring came that year, they noticed no one had trimmed the trees. Lem would never let his beloved trees go and not take care of them. Finally, the widow Jones's children who were grown into fine young men by now went to try and find Lem.

They found his cabin and his wood pile. They knocked and then entered his cabin. Lem was nowhere to be found. Inside the cabin they found Lem's knives all sharpened and neatly laid out ready to use. They found lots of carvings of all kinds of animals, little carved houses, and carvings of himself with his long beard. They also found a beautiful life-sized carving of Lem and Toby. It was perfect in every detail. It must have taken a long time to carve it and it was carved all from one piece of wood.

Lem's carrying sack and jacket hung behind the door. No one ever knew what happened to Lem. Maybe he just went off into his beloved Ozark Mountains or maybe, is that his spirit in that life-sized carving?

LEM'S MUSEUM

When people found out his carvings were no longer available, they began to clammer for them and soon they were very scarce. The widow Jones's son remembered all the critters and other things that Lem had carved for them. They knew they would never sell, as they were so special to them, so they opened a museum and filled it with Lem's carvings. The life-sized carving of Lem and Toby is the main attraction. It had to be put behind glass as it seemed everyone who saw it wanted to touch it, like it contained some sort of magic. People come from miles around to visit the museum, and it has become the main attraction in the town. The widow Jones remembered Lem's words and named their museum "I Told You So." Many folks have written down their stories of Lem and how he helped them.

They say sometimes late at night, you can hear Lem's laughter echo through the museum. Lem was never seen again, but through the museum, his carvings and all the people he helped will never be forgotten. People have been said to have seen an old man and his dog at times in the Ozarks. Then again, maybe that is just talk. Do you think so?

The End.